TO_____

SMALL WORLD LIBRARY

THE TREASURE ISLANDS
An Adventure in Denmark

GROLIER ENTERPRISES INC.
DANBURY, CONNECTICUT

© The Walt Disney Company. All rights reserved.
Printed in the United States of America.
Developed by The Walt Disney Company in conjunction with Nancy Hall, Inc.
Originally published in Denmark by Egmont Books.
ISBN: 0-7172-8433-6

It was Mickey and Goofy's first trip to Copenhagen, Denmark's capital city. The tour bus had just let them off at Town Hall Square.

"Everything is so beautiful here!" Mickey said.

"So clean, too!" added Goofy. "And the people seem friendly! Look at all the happy bicyclists!"

"It was nice of your Uncle Ole to invite us," said Mickey.

"It sure was," agreed Goofy. "But I wish he had given us his address instead of this drawing."

Goofy and Mickey stared at the drawing Uncle Ole had tucked inside his letter. It was a picture of a fish with long, blonde hair! Written on the bottom of the drawing were the words, "Find me!"

   Mickey and Goofy walked along Stroget, a winding
street that stretches across the city. Stroget is famous
for its wonderful shops and fancy fountains.
   As they walked Mickey laughed and said, "Maybe
we can find a pet shop that sells fish. Who knows?
Maybe in Denmark all the goldfish have hair!"

"Gawrsh, look!" cried Goofy, stopping to stare at a display of jewelry. "Those rocks sure are pretty."

"Those aren't really rocks," Mickey told him. "That's amber. It's the hardened sap of trees that grew millions of years ago. Denmark is known for its amber. And for its silversmiths, too," he added, pointing to a window filled with beautiful objects made of silver.

By the time the two had reached a part of the city known as Nyhavn, or "New Harbor," they were ready for something to eat. Goofy spied the perfect place to sample some of Denmark's delicious red hot dogs.

"Let's walk by the harbor," said Mickey. "The ocean is the best place to look for fish, with or without hair."

Although they didn't find the fish they were searching for, they did see the sights in Nyhavn. The lively port was filled with fine ships and charming buildings. Some of the buildings were over three hundred years old.

After a while, Mickey and Goofy decided to continue exploring the harbor by boat. But when they got to the dock, the tour boat had just left.

"Gawrsh!" cried Goofy. "What do we do now?"

Just then a fishing boat pulled up to the dock. The captain and his granddaughter stepped out.

"My name is Lene," said the girl with a smile.

"I'm Captain Hans," said the man. "Welcome to Denmark. You look lost. Can we help?"

Goofy explained that they had come to Denmark to visit his uncle. Then he showed the strange picture to Captain Hans.

"Have you ever seen a fish like this?" asked Goofy.

The jolly old captain chuckled. "I certainly have," he replied. "I can take you to her right now!"

Because Denmark is a country made up of hundreds of islands, the best way to get around is by boat. So Mickey and Goofy climbed aboard.

"We'll have you there in no time," said Captain Hans as he steered the boat out of the harbor.

It wasn't long before they were pulling into another
harbor. Lene tugged on Goofy's sleeve and pointed.
"See, Goofy," she cried, "that's what you've been
looking for!"

Sure enough, there in the middle of the harbor sat The Little Mermaid. The statue, dedicated to the famous Danish storyteller Hans Christian Andersen, represents one of his most beloved characters.

"Gawrsh!" cried Goofy. "You must be right."

But Goofy was confused. "I don't understand," he said. Do you think Uncle Ole sent us on a wild-goose chase?"

"Or some kind of treasure hunt," said Mickey excitedly. "Look!"

He carefully climbed over the slippery rocks and retrieved another drawing hidden near the statue. It was a picture of an ancient Danish warrior called a Viking . . . a sleeping Viking!

Lene looked at the picture and giggled.

"Oh, here in Denmark everyone knows him. My grandfather can take you to him, if you'd like."

"Uh, I don't know," said Goofy, nervously staring at the fierce-looking warrior. "Are you sure he'd want us to bother him?"

"Come on," said Mickey. "We can't quit now."

Before he knew it, Goofy was headed for Kronborg, a famous castle in the city of Helsingor.

Lene led Mickey and Goofy to the castle's dungeon. She pointed to a statue. "His name is Holger Danske," Lene explained. "A legend says if Denmark is ever in trouble, Holger will wake up and rescue us."

Goofy stared at the huge Viking and gulped.

"Uh . . . I feel safer already!" he said.

Just then Mickey discovered another drawing behind the Viking's shield. "It's a picture of a strangely carved stone," he said. "What could it mean?"

"I know just where to find that stone," said Lene.

"Come on," said Captain Hans. "It's not very far by train."

"Maybe the stone's pure gold and we'll all be rich," said Goofy dreamily.

It wasn't long before the little group arrived at a huge outdoor museum called Lejre (Lie-ruh).

"This place was built to look like a Danish village of two thousand years ago," explained Captain Hans.

Mickey and Goofy watched in amazement as workers dressed in copies of clothing from the iron age showed their visitors how people in Denmark used to make pots, repair wagons, and weave cloth. Goofy admired some long buildings.

"Those are called long houses," said Lene. "Vikings lived in them with their families and even their animals!"

Captain Hans led Goofy to a display featuring a strangely carved stone.

"Here's the stone in your drawing," he said. "It's called a rune stone. Our Viking ancestors had no paper, so they had to write their letters on rocks."

"Gawrsh!" said Goofy. "I'd hate to have been a mail carrier in those days!"

"Look!" cried Mickey. "There's another drawing under the stone." It showed a tower on a hilltop.

Lene whispered to her grandfather, and soon they were heading for western Denmark on an antique steamboat. As they sailed, Mickey and Goofy admired the beautiful farmlands dotted with windmills.

Before long the four friends arrived at the base of a big hill called Himmelbjerget (Him-ul-bair-ged), which means "Sky Mountain."

"This is one of our tallest hills," said Lene.

"I'm glad it's not too high," said Goofy. "I'm tired."

Captain Hans chuckled. "Denmark is a flat country," he said.

At the top, Mickey and Goofy looked at the imposing tower. They searched and searched, but they found no treasure. There were no more drawings either.

"Gawrsh!" cried Goofy. "I guess there is no treasure!"

Just then a figure stepped out from inside the tower. It was Goofy's Uncle Ole!

Uncle Ole gave his nephew a welcoming hug and said with a chuckle, "No treasure, Goofy? Are you absolutely sure?"

Uncle Ole pointed to the breathtaking landscape below.

"Haven't you found treasure everywhere you've been on your tour of our beautiful islands?"

Goofy thought for a moment. "I see what you mean, Uncle Ole."

"These really are the Treasure Islands," agreed Mickey with a smile.

The next day Uncle Ole took Mickey, Goofy, and their friends to a famous amusement park in Copenhagen called Tivoli Gardens. As they made their way through the beautiful park, Goofy stopped to try out every ride in sight!

Uncle Ole treated them all to a traditional Danish lunch. Mickey and Goofy thought everything was

delicious, especially the big meatballs called *frikadeller.*

"Thank you for everything," Mickey said to Uncle Ole. "You made our trip to Denmark an adventure we'll never forget."

"Gawrsh! That's for sure!" added Goofy. "You can send me on a wild-goose chase anytime!"

Did You Know...?

Every country has many different customs and places that make it special. Some of the things that make Denmark special are mentioned below. Do you recognize any of them from the story?

The swan is often a symbol of Denmark. One of Hans Christian Andersen's most famous fairy tales, "The Ugly Duckling," is about a swan.

Andersen also wrote "The Princess and the Pea," "The Emperor's New Clothes," and "The Little Mermaid." Have you read any of his stories?

There are thousands of miles of special paths all over Denmark just for bicycles. About three-quarters of Denmark's five million people own bicycles. Many ride their bikes to work instead of using cars.

Soccer is popular in Denmark. For some games, fans wear red and white, the colors of the Danish flag.

Danes are expert bakers.
One type of pastry they
make is famous in the
United States, where it is
called Danish pastry.
But the Danes call the same
pastry Vienna bread, after
Vienna, the capital of
Austria. So what do the
Austrians call it?

Like the people of Holland, the Danes have used
windmills and the power of the wind to grind their
wheat into flour for hundreds of years.

Now the Danes build windmills that make
electricity. Danes export more windmills than anybody
in the whole world.

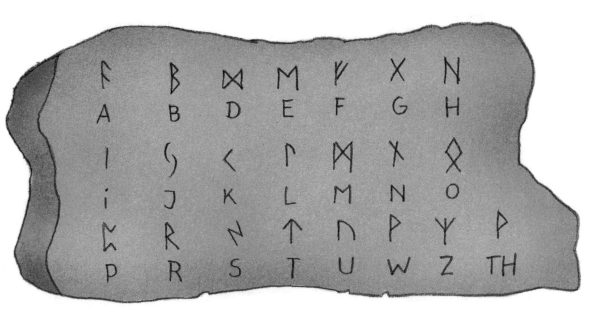

More than a thousand years ago, the Danes and their close neighbors had their own alphabet called Runic. Here it is printed above the letters of our alphabet. Can you use Runic letters to spell your name?

Over two hundred years ago, Danes opened the first amusement park in the world. There children and their parents picnicked, went on rides, and played games.

The park is called Bakken, which means "the hill." It's still open every summer. Imagine, more than 200 years of fun!